THE CLUB

STEPHANIE WATSON

NIGHT FALL

THE CLUB

STEPHANIE WATSON

MINNEAPOLIS

Darby Creek
A division of Lerner Publishing Group, Inc.
241 First Avenue North
Minneapolis, MN 55401 U.S.A.

Website address: www.lernerbooks.com

Cover design: Emily Love
Cover photograph: iStockphoto; Henk Badenhorst/
iStockphoto

Watson, Stephanie, 1969–
The club / by Stephanie Watson.
p. cm. — (Night fall)
ISBN 978-0-7613-6147-3 (lib. bdg. : alk. paper)
[1. Horror stories.] I. Title.
PZ7.W32949Cl 2010
[Fic]—dc22   2010003061

Manufactured in the United States of America
1–BP–7/15/10

To my son, Jake.
No matter how many books I write, you will always be my greatest creation.

*Deep into that darkness peering, long I stood there
   wondering, fearing,
Doubting, dreaming dreams no mortal ever dared
   to dream before*

—*Edgar Allan Poe,* The Raven

osh took a deep breath. It was the Bridgewater High championship football game. The bright stadium lights shone all around him. He could hear his classmates cheering in the stands. All he had to do was kick a field goal and they would win the championship. But as he readied himself for the kick, he felt a firm tap on his shoulder.

Josh turned. Standing next to him was his teammate Ned. Josh gasped at the sight. Ned was bruised and covered with blood. His football uniform was just a shred of cloth. His left arm hung from his body as if it were coming off. Deep gashes cut into his arms. He stared at Josh with bulging, bloodshot eyes.

"Oh my God," Josh whispered. On the left side of Ned's chest, blood oozed from a gaping hole. Ned smiled, and blood rushed from his mouth, spilling down his neck and onto his marred chest. He choked on the blood, laughing.

"Josh . . ." Ned moaned like an animal. "I have something for you, pal." Ned reached out his right hand to Josh. In it was Ned's beating heart. He pressed the slimy organ into Josh's palm.

Josh screamed as he watched the heart writhe in his hand.

Josh woke up. He was screaming into the hot air. His heart was pounding furiously. *It was just a dream. It was just a dream,* he told himself over and over as he tried to catch his breath. But Josh knew that it wasn't just any dream. He had to do something to stop the nightmares. He had to stop the chain of innocent deaths. He couldn't believe that only two short weeks had passed since he first joined the Club. . . .

"ey New Yawk! Your Giants suck! Up here we know how to play football." Ned Onger punctuated that brilliant statement by smacking Josh hard on one shoulder.

Josh tried to edge past Ned, but the linebacker's massive frame blocked his path. Josh had been going to Bridgewater High for just a week, and already he was being picked on. He didn't understand it. No one at his old high school had picked on him. What was the big deal with being from New York anyway?

Josh was used to moving a lot. His father was

relocated often because of his job. But Josh had been at his last school almost two years. That was the longest he had ever stayed at one school. He'd had a lot of friends and even a girlfriend for a little while. He had wanted so badly to finish high school there. Then, just two weeks into his senior year, it was time to pack up again. And so far, Bridgewater High was a far cry from his old school.

"Are you ready to humiliate yourself at Friday's football tryouts?" Ned asked, still blocking Josh's path.

"Can't wait," Josh said sarcastically. Josh knew it was stupid to even try out. He had really liked playing football at his old school, even though he wasn't a star like Ned. But with the competition at Bridgewater, it was a long shot that Josh would even make the team.

Ned just laughed as he shoved Josh into the lockers. Josh's books spilled everywhere.

"Gonna have to block better if you want to be on *our* team!" Ned yelled over his shoulder as he went to join his friends. They were all laughing.

Josh groaned as he leaned over to retrieve his

books. Life was so unfair. How come someone so mean and stupid was the one who had so much talent on the football field?

Josh sighed as he walked to his next class. It was only Monday. How would he ever survive another week at this stupid school?

Later that day, Josh was walking through the cafeteria when someone slammed hard against his right side.

"Watch it!" someone yelled. Josh steadied his tray of spaghetti and turned to see who had run into him.

It was Sabina Lawston. Josh had noticed Sabina on his first day at Bridgewater High. It was hard not to. Sabina always wore black clothes, and her hair was dyed bright pink. Sabina was also one of the smartest girls in the school. Everyone tried to get her to do their homework, but Sabina always refused.

"Sorry, Sabina," Josh said. "Are you okay?"

Sabina brushed off her black sweatshirt. She looked up at him, "Oh hey, you're the new guy. The New Yorker? Joe, right?"

Josh frowned. "Yeah. It's Josh, actually." He turned to find a table to eat lunch at, expecting to sit by himself. His first day at Bridgewater, he'd made the fatal mistake of sitting at Ned Onger's table. Ned had looked pretty pleased with himself as he spilled Josh's tray onto his lap. After that, Josh had tried to sit with a few of the other groups. They hadn't been especially welcoming either.

"Hey." Sabina was still behind him. "Why don't you sit with me and my friends today?"

"Really?" asked Josh.

Sabina led him to a table where two guys were already sitting. "This is Dan Chissolm." Sabina gestured to the guy to her right. He was very tall and extremely thin, with dark, wavy hair and bad skin. At the moment, Dan had his head buried in a PlayStation Portable. He briefly lifted his head and one hand in greeting before going back to his game.

"And this is Jackson Winder," Sabina said, pointing across from her.

"Hey," Jackson said in a whispering voice. Jackson was short with blond hair and large blue eyes—or maybe his out-of-date glasses just made them look that way. He gave Josh a warm smile.

"Hi, guys," Josh said. "Thanks for letting me sit with you. It's been a lonely week since I started here."

"Get used to it. Don't expect the vipers at this school to roll out the red carpet for you," Dan grumbled without lifting his head from his game.

"Don't be such a cynic, Dan. There are some nice kids here." Jackson was obviously one of those glass-half-full kind of guys.

"Like us," Sabina said, smiling.

"Like you," Josh agreed. Josh was starting to like Sabina. She was nicer to him than anyone else at Bridgewater had been. He realized he was staring at her when she blushed.

"Oh my God," Sabina said after a minute. "I have such a headache. Lindsey is driving me crazy!"

"Uh-oh," Dan said, putting his video game aside. "Trouble in chemistry?"

Sabina turned to Josh. "Lindsey Steele is my lab partner in chemistry. She is not doing *any* of the work. I have to get an A in that class. It's the only way I'll get a scholarship to Harvard." Sabina stabbed at her spaghetti with her fork. "My mom could never afford Harvard."

"Oh, that sucks," said Josh. He was impressed that Sabina was even thinking about Harvard. "Which one is Lindsey Steele?"

Jackson pointed to the table where most of the football players and dance-team girls ate lunch. Lindsey was tall and had dark, wavy hair. She was laughing at one of the guys who was throwing peanuts at another table. Lindsey looked like she could be a swimsuit model.

"She's a pain," Sabina said. "Her family has tons of money. She doesn't have to worry about scholarships. But no way she's gonna cost me my A in chemistry! I stayed late yesterday to finish *our* lab assignment myself."

"Oh, was that why I saw you leaving at four?" said Jackson. He talked so quietly Josh could barely hear him.

"Yeah," said Sabina. "How did debate practice go for you?"

Josh was surprised. He couldn't imagine Jackson performing a debate speech with that voice.

Jackson shrugged. "Okay. I still can't match up with Miles Danforth."

"Ugh," Dan groaned. "Stop comparing yourself to that dude. He's a jerk, anyway."

"Yeah," Jackson murmured. "But he rocks at debate." Jackson's eyes lowered to the carton of milk in front of him.

"So, are you going to stay after school again today?" Dan asked Sabina.

"No," said Sabina. "I need a break. Do you guys want to come over to my house?"

"I have to be home by five. Mark—" Dan turned to Josh. "That's my loser stepfather. He wants to have dinner before he goes to work, assuming he isn't drunk again. But I can come over for a while." He didn't sound enthusiastic. Jackson just nodded.

"Cool," Sabina said. "I found this really cool-looking old game in my basement this weekend. I thought we might play it."

"Is it Tetris?" Dan asked, looking up at her.

"No. . . ."

"Ms. Pac-Man? Asteroids?"

"No, Dan. It's not a video game. It's a board game. It looks almost like a Ouija board, but it has something to do with witchcraft."

"Sounds spooky!" said Jackson with a smile.

"You should come too, Josh," said Sabina.

"Sure!" Josh agreed. By now, he would have walked over a cliff if Sabina had asked him to.

After school, Sabina and Josh walked to her house. Even from the end of Sparrow Drive, Josh could tell that it was really old. The tiny, red, wood-framed house looked like it was from colonial times. On their way over, Sabina had explained that the house had been in her family for generations.

Sabina's mom was still at work, so Josh and Sabina grabbed a couple cans of soda and a bag of cookies and headed downstairs. Josh felt his body go cold as he went down the dark, wooden staircase. Something about Sabina's basement made him want to keep his back to the wall. He felt like someone might sneak up on him. Even with the odd pieces of 1970s-style furniture scattered around, the basement was still pretty creepy. Underneath a few assorted throw rugs, the wood floor looked ancient and dusty. Cobwebs stretched everywhere across the brick walls.

"It's kind of creepy down here," Josh mentioned casually. He didn't want Sabina to think he was a wimp.

"You feel it too?" Sabina looked at him with wide eyes. They both shivered. "Yeah, I never come down here alone. But it's a good setting for our game."

Sabina and Josh plopped down in a couple of red beanbag chairs by an old wooden coffee table. Josh shifted from side to side, trying to shake off the eerie feeling. Sabina kept looking over her shoulders and crossing her arms around herself.

While they waited for Dan and Jackson, Josh distracted himself by telling Sabina stories about a few of his past schools, including his last high school—Wentworth Academy in New York. He'd been in the same classroom as the reality-TV star Jeremy Fresh (his real name was Jeremy Finstermacher, but that didn't sound nearly as cool).

Sabina's eyes widened. "Really? What was he like?" She leaned in closer to Josh. She smelled good, like lilacs or something like that.

"About as dumb as a bag of nails. Whenever our calculus teacher used to call on him, Jeremy would pretend to drop his pencil. Then he'd spend five minutes scrambling around on the floor trying to find it."

"I'm not surprised," Sabina laughed. They were so caught up in their conversation that they didn't hear the sound of footsteps creaking down the basement stairs.

"Well, isn't this cozy," said Dan as he bent down to clear the ceiling at the bottom of the stairs. Josh thought he detected some jealousy in Dan's voice.

"Hey guys." Josh heard Jackson's breathy voice from behind Dan. Jackson looked pretty pale. Maybe he didn't like Sabina's basement either.

Dan and Jackson each grabbed a couple of cookies and sat down on an old flowered couch on the other side of the coffee table.

"So, where is this game you wanted to show us?" Dan asked, looking slightly bored.

"Oh yeah, let me get it." Sabina opened a small closet door on the other side of the basement and rummaged around. After a minute or so, she reemerged with a long, dusty box. "I was cleaning out a bunch of my old art supplies when I found this way in the back."

She pushed the bag of cookies aside and put the game down on the table. Its cover was black and marked with a large pentagram—the symbol of witchcraft. Underneath the symbol were the words *Black Magic.* The game looked decades old, if not more. Although it was just a wooden game board, there was something ghostly about it. Josh felt strange—was he breathing faster than usual? And why did it feel like something was squeezing his stomach? Suddenly, Josh wasn't sure if he wanted to play.

The game didn't come with instructions," Sabina said. She placed the dark wooden game board in the middle of their circle. "But there are a bunch of spell cards." Sabina pulled out the yellowing, faded cards to show her friends. "Each of them has a different spell. They also have numbers on them. I think that shows how many spaces you move around the board. But some of the numbers are negative. That's for the bad spells. They move you backward. The one who gets to the end first wins."

Josh looked at a few of the spell cards. They were things like "To Find Something Lost" or "Turn Your Cat into a Horse." The negative spells were a bit more intense, like "Give Your Enemy a Green Nose." But they were all silly in some form or another.

Dan yawned. "Sounds like a game my little sister would play."

"You're right, there isn't much to it. But then I found this crystal and another set of spells." Sabina lifted a long, thin crystal. When she held it up, it bent the light, creating a rainbow of colors. Josh thought he saw something else in the crystal. He leaned closer to examine it.

It looked like a girl's face. Her mouth was open like she was screaming in pain. Josh gasped. The girl looked so real, like she was alive. But Sabina quickly lifted the crystal away.

"Are you okay, Josh?" she asked.

"Dude." Dan laughed nervously. "What's wrong?"

Josh realized that his whole body was shaking. He took several deep breaths and tried to calm down. Of course there wasn't a girl inside the crystal! He was just creeped out by a stupid basement in an old house. He didn't want his new friends to think he was a complete pansy. He shook his head and forced a laugh.

"Oh, it's nothing," he said. "Just a little chilly down here, I guess!"

Dan raised his eyebrows and let out an exasperated sigh.

"Next to the crystal I found a handwritten note with the other spells." Sabina held out a piece of faded paper with fancy script. "Someone who played the game must have added it. It says, 'Choose one of these special spells. Rub the crystal. Think of someone who has wronged you. You will reverse the force of their evil and send good spirits your way.'" These spells sounded much more sinister to Josh. "There's Nightmare, Transformation, Thought Control, Dark Mirror . . ." Sabina read off the cards.

Dan snorted. "So, we rub this crystal and hex our enemies? Sounds realistic."

"I think it sounds pretty cool," Jackson said, reaching for the cards and thumbing through them.

Then Jackson pointed to some scribbled writing in the corner of the board. "What's that?"

Sabina lowered her head to read the script. "It's hard to make out," she said. "I think it says, 'Beware all who play. Death awaits.'"

"Boo!" yelled Dan. Sabina shrieked. Josh laughed. He was starting to calm down a little. It *was* just a game, after all.

"Let's try some spells!" Sabina said.

"Let's do the hexing thing," Jackson suggested. "That sounded kind of interesting."

"Yeah, awesome!" Sabina agreed.

Dan laughed. "Like you have anyone to hex, Sabina. Everyone is nice to you." Dan looked away from the group. Josh wondered who wasn't nice to Dan.

"Oh yeah?" Sabina challenged. "I'd totally hex Lindsey Steele! She's been stressing me out so bad!"

"Let's do it then!" Jackson said.

"I'm up for it," Josh agreed. Why not? It sounded fun.

Sabina dimmed the lights, leaving the four of them in almost total darkness. Josh felt a slight twinge of panic, but there was no way he was going to show it. The crystal seemed to sparkle in the darkness. Josh thought he could still see the faint, unnerving outline of a girl in its center. He tried not to look at it.

Sabina, Josh, Dan, and Jackson sat in a small circle on the carpet with the crystal and spell cards in the middle.

"So, how do we do this?" Josh asked. "Do we say the spell and name of the person out loud, or do we just think about them?"

Sabina looked at the old piece of paper again. "It says, 'Think of someone who has wronged you.' I'd say we whisper the name of the person and the spell and then concentrate on them in our minds."

Josh nodded. It probably didn't matter how they played the game. It wasn't like it was going to do anything.

"I'll start," Sabina said, shuffling through the deck and finally fishing out a card. "Lindsey Steele," she whispered. "Transformation."

Jackson went next. "Miles Danforth . . . Voice of Steel."

"Mark Nelson . . . Fantasy Maker," said Dan.

"That's his stepdad," Sabina whispered to Josh.

Finally, it was Josh's turn. He looked through the remaining cards and chose one. "Ned Onger . . . Dark Mirror," he whispered. No one deserved to be hexed more than that guy.

Josh put the crystal in the middle of the board. Suddenly, the crystal began to glow brighter and brighter.

"What the—?" Josh heard Dan say. The crystal flashed brightly. Then it went dark, and a terrified scream filled the room. It reminded Josh of when his brother's cat had been hit by a car and dragged for a couple of blocks.

"What *was* that?" Dan yelled. He was groping for

the light on the wall. Sabina got to it first, and light flooded the room.

"I don't know!" she said. Josh could tell she was trying to act calm. "Maybe there are batteries in the game or something?"

"It's way too old for that," said Jackson. He looked even paler than usual.

"Something outside then?" Sabina offered.

"Yeah," Josh agreed. He was trying to stay as cool as Sabina. "Like an animal being attacked. Maybe it was a rabbit?"

"A rabbit? That was no rabbit!" Dan argued.

"Is it cold in here?" Sabina asked. Josh could feel her shivering next to him. It *had* gotten cold. So cold, in fact, that Josh could see Sabina's breath. "This house is so old and the insulation is so bad that it's always either too hot or too cold in here," she complained.

"It's almost seventy degrees outside! How can it be *this* cold in here?" Dan asked.

Sabina shrugged. Josh looked down at the crystal in the center of the board again. He could still see the girl. Only now it looked like she was crying.

That night, Josh could not stop thinking about Black Magic. He could still picture the crying girl inside the crystal. The whole thing was freaky. But still, Josh felt a strong desire to play the game again. What was that about?

Right before he went to bed, he got a call from Sabina. "Hey," she said. "The guys want to play the game again tomorrow. Are you in?"

"Sure!" Josh was surprised to hear himself agree.

"Okay." She lowered her voice. "But don't bring anyone else . . . just the four of us, okay?"

Josh agreed. For some reason, he didn't want anyone else to be in on the game, either.

For the rest of the week Sabina, Josh, Dan, and Jackson met almost every day after school to play Black Magic. They never tried out any other spell cards. Instead they repeated the ritual exactly as they had the first time. Josh didn't know why he never felt like trying another spell. He just didn't. Josh also started to enjoy the eerie feeling that the game always gave him. He still saw the girl's face in the crystal every time they played, but it bothered him less and less. In fact, if Josh missed even a day of hanging out to play Black Magic, he couldn't stop thinking about it until he played again. The others didn't like playing unless all four players could attend. The four of them started referring to themselves as "The Club."

Sabina slammed her lunch tray down on the table, making Josh and the other guys jump.

"Jeez, Sabina," complained Dan. "What's wrong?"

But Josh knew nothing was wrong at all. In fact, Sabina was smiling broadly. She laughed at Dan and gave him a playful punch in the shoulder.

"Nothing!" Sabina exclaimed. Josh noticed that Sabina could barely sit still. "Guess what?" She beamed at them.

"You killed Lindsey?" Dan joked.

"No, better!"

"Well, hurry up and tell us," Dan said. "Because I have some pretty awesome news to share too!"

"Let's hear it!" Jackson suddenly piped up. Josh nearly fell out of his chair. He'd never heard Jackson speak so loudly.

"My mom got a promotion! She'll make twice her salary!" Sabina exclaimed. "I'm going to get to go to Harvard. In fact, they sent me a letter yesterday practically *begging* me to apply. Can you believe that? I got letters from Yale and Cornell too!"

"That's awesome!" Josh exclaimed. It was great to see her so happy. If anyone deserved to go to Harvard, it was Sabina.

"So, Dan," Sabina asked after she'd calmed down a little bit. "What's your news?"

"I got an e-mail last night from Video Arts," Dan said. His grin was so big it looked like it was about to escape from his face.

Sabina gasped. "The video game developer?"

"The very one. One of their lead designers read my video game blog on 'The Game Guide.' I wrote about my idea for a new game called Speed Attack. Tricked-out cars shoot at each other while racing around different kinds of tracks."

"And?" Sabina leaned across the table.

"He loved it so much he convinced his manager to buy the concept! They're going to produce *my* video game!"

Sabina shrieked and ran around to give Dan a hug.

"That's amazing, Dan. I can't wait to play it," Josh said.

"Awesome!" exclaimed Jackson.

"Well," Josh said as they finished up their lunches. "I hope your good luck rubs off on me. I have football tryouts tonight."

"Good luck!" Sabina said. Josh smiled. He was pretty sure he wasn't going to make the team, but it was nice to have friends who would cheer him on.

"Club meeting tonight?" asked Dan.

"Sure," Josh said. He'd been thinking about playing Black Magic all day. The others nodded eagerly.

As Josh got up to head to class, Lindsey Steele glided over to the table. Lindsey always walked like she had wheels instead of feet.

"Hey, *Sabrina*," Lindsey said as she approached.

Josh could tell Sabina was trying not to roll her eyes. "It's *Sabina*," she said.

Lindsey scratched at her arm a little bit. Josh noticed that she looked different today, but he couldn't figure out what it was at first. Then he realized—she was wearing a heavy turtleneck sweater. Usually her shirts were much more revealing. Then Josh noticed angry red welts just under her collar. Dan must have noticed them too.

"What's the matter, Lindsey? Got fleas?" Dan asked.

She shot him an evil look. "I'm having an allergic reaction, as if it's any of *your* business." She turned to Sabina, "I just wanted to ask you if chemistry is in the lab today."

"Yes, it is," Sabina said.

"Okay, thanks." As Lindsey reached up to scratch her neck, Josh noticed welts on her hands too. There were also a few red spots on the sides of her face, which looked flushed. She shot one more annoyed look at Dan and hurried away.

"Feel better, Lindsey!" Sabina shouted after her. Then Sabina turned to the guys. "I've been her lab partner all semester. . . . You'd think she'd know my name!"

As Josh stepped off the football field Friday afternoon, he felt like he might just take off into the sky. He'd made the football team! He'd kicked his best field goal ever. Coach Tyree had been just as amazed as Josh. Coach even said that Josh might have a chance to play for a college team someday. Ned Onger had looked like he was going to faint right there on the field. Josh had to admit that it felt pretty great to make Ned look like an amateur, especially after all the crap Ned put him through.

Josh went to his car, picturing himself snagging

college football scholarships and playing in the NFL, when a loud voice interrupted him.

"Wait up, Josh!" Josh turned to see Jackson running after him. Jackson was breathless when he caught up with Josh.

"Are you okay, Jackson?" Josh asked. Josh felt a sinking feeling in his stomach. Jackson's face looked more pale than usual. Maybe he'd run too hard.

"I'm . . . great . . . ," Jackson said between gasps of air. "Well, at least . . . I think I'm great. I'm not sure. Can I ride with you to Sabina's?"

"Sure," Josh said.

In the car, Jackson kept fidgeting.

"So, what's up, Jackson?" Josh was actually dying to tell him about his football triumph, but Jackson still looked kind of woozy around the eyes.

"Do you hear me?" Jackson asked. "My voice . . . it's *loud.*"

Jackson *did* sound a lot louder today than he had at the beginning of the week. Josh just thought Jackson was getting more comfortable around him.

"I didn't do anything," Jackson said. "I'm not

trying to talk louder. I mean, I'm rocking at debate . . . it's like my voice just completely changed."

"Dude, maybe you're finally going through puberty," Josh teased. But Jackson didn't seem to think it was funny.

"Everyone in my family is soft-spoken." Jackson lowered his head a little. "And there's something else too."

"What?" Josh asked.

"It's Miles Danforth." Jackson swallowed. "Something is wrong with his voice."

By the time they reached Sabina's house, Josh had heard the whole story from Jackson. Apparently, Miles and Jackson had been opponents during a practice debate that afternoon. Miles had completely choked. While Jackson spoke loudly and clearly, Miles had been unable to speak at all. He was clutching his throat and coughing. No one could figure out what had happened. Miles was the school's top debater. In the end, Miles's mother had had to come pick him up from school.

"Let's just play Black Magic," Josh said, walking up Sabina's front steps. "I mean, I'm sure a doctor will figure out what's wrong with Miles."

"Yeah." Jackson followed reluctantly. "It's just weird. I gained a voice. . . . He lost his."

"I think it's called irony," Josh replied. Jackson didn't look convinced.

"And Lindsey has that rash . . . ," Jackson muttered.

Just then Sabina burst through the front door. She had her purse in hand and a pile of chemistry textbooks under the other arm. Her pink hair was sticking out in all directions, and she had only one arm inside her coat.

"Josh!" she exclaimed, seeing him and Jackson on the steps. "I'm glad you guys are here. Can you drive me to the hospital?"

"Yeah, sure," Josh said. "What's wrong?"

"It's nothing really," Sabina said. But Josh could tell something was up. "Lindsey Steele is in the hospital. I have to bring her some chemistry homework."

"What's wrong with her? Is it the rash?" Jackson asked as Sabina fumbled to lock the front door.

"I . . . I don't know," Sabina answered.

"Where's Dan? Wasn't he going to meet here earlier?" Josh asked. He just realized that Dan was late.

"I don't know! He never showed up." Sabina shrugged to balance the pile of books in her arm. She ran to Josh's car. "Let's go!"

9

Sabina rode shotgun, telling Josh where to turn during the fifteen-minute ride to County Hospital. Jackson was quiet for most of the ride. When they got there, Sabina asked at the front desk for Lindsey's room number—560—and they headed for the elevator.

The elevator door was just about to close. Josh stuck a hand inside the doors. The door opened up again to reveal Miles Danforth standing with a woman who must have been his mother.

"Hey, Miles," said Jackson. Josh felt shaky looking

at Miles. Miles's face was pale, with a green tint to it. His eyes were sunken into their sockets. His neck looked red and swollen.

Miles just glared at Jackson.

"Are you a friend of Miles's?" asked Mrs. Danforth.

"Sort of," Jackson murmured.

"Miles has lost his voice," Mrs. Danforth explained. Jackson shot a look at Josh that said *I told you so.* "We've been passed around from doctor to doctor all afternoon, but no one knows what's wrong. It's so odd, but when they tested his throat, they found this strange, metallic substance. The doctors have absolutely no idea what it is. They've never seen anything like it before."

Now, Sabina looked worried. "Well, we hope you get better soon, Miles," she said. As Miles and his mother got off the elevator, Sabina rubbed her eyes. Josh knew she had to be thinking about Lindsey.

When they arrived at Lindsey's room, they found her door guarded by a man in a hazmat suit. The thick yellow suit covered his entire body. He wore a face mask and thick goggles. What the hell was going on? Josh glanced at Sabina, but she was focusing in on the guard.

"Whoa! Whoa!" the hazmat guy called out as they approached. "No visitors!"

"It's okay," Sabina said. "Lindsey knows me. I just have homework for her."

"Family only," the man answered. "Trust me. You don't want to get what she has."

Just then, a woman emerged from the room. She was wearing a hazmat suit too. When she removed her goggles and mask, Josh could see that she was weeping. When she saw Jackson, Josh, and Sabina, more tears spilled down her cheeks.

"Are you Lindsey's friends?" she asked. "I'm her mother." Mrs. Steele looked like an older version of her daughter—tall, brunette, and with the same perfect, upturned nose.

Sabina just stared at Mrs. Steele. Josh could feel her shaking next to him.

"Um," Josh managed. "Sort of. We brought her homework."

"The doctors don't know what's wrong with her," Mrs. Steele croaked. "They think it's some kind of virus, but they've never seen anything like it." Her chest heaved with the sobs she was trying to hold inside. "It's tearing holes through her. I could see almost all the way inside her." She put a hand to her mouth and gagged slightly.

The door opened again, and a doctor came out wearing the same kind of head-to-toe protective suit as Mrs. Steele. He looked grim.

Josh couldn't help himself. In the few seconds that the door was open, he craned his head to get a look inside. Immediately he wished he hadn't. From the terrified look on Sabina's face, he knew that she had seen what he'd seen too.

The right side of Lindsey's face looked as perfect as ever. But when she turned her head toward Josh, all he could see was a mess of raw, rotting flesh. It looked like something was eating her—from the inside out.

On the ride home from the hospital everyone was really quiet. Josh knew that they did not want to admit what they were thinking. Was it their fault? Had Sabina's and Jackson's hexes on Lindsey and Miles actually worked? And what about all the amazing stuff they'd been experiencing? Did the game cause that too? Then there was the guilt. All Josh wanted to do was play the game even more.

When they drove up to Sabina's house, Sabina gasped. A large, shadowy figure loomed in the darkness. Josh turned into the driveway. It was Dan, standing in the glare of the headlights like an angry ghost.

Where the hell have you guys been?" Dan asked as they were getting out of the car.

"The hospital," Sabina murmured. "Where have you been?"

"I was late because I had to call the cops!" Dan yelled. Josh suddenly felt his blood run cold. "I found Ned Onger bleeding on the sidewalk on my way home from school. I guess some thugs really beat him down. Had some major stab wounds too. Don't know if he'll live."

Josh felt dizzy. He leaned over, bracing his hands on his knees. *What have I done?* he thought.

"This is getting way too creepy," Sabina said.

"What's way too creepy?" Dan asked. Josh had to feel for the guy. He had no idea what the game had set in motion. They explained what had happened to Lindsey and Miles and now Ned. Dan looked sort of surprised, but he didn't look as worried as Josh felt. Josh could tell Dan craved to play the game the same way he did.

"It's just coincidence," Dan said with a shrug. "We know it isn't real magic. I mean, who believes in that stuff? You guys aren't seriously telling me you think we did this? Come on." Dan was almost laughing.

"I know it sounds crazy, but it's just . . ." Tears were filling Sabina's eyes.

"Dan," Josh tried. "You didn't see Lindsey. . . . It was awful."

"Yeah, well, I saw Ned," Dan reasoned. "Sometimes bad stuff just happens to people. It's not our fault. Plus, I hexed Mark and not a thing has happened to that jerk!"

"Not yet," Jackson mumbled.

"Do you guys want to play Black Magic tonight or what?" Dan crossed his arms over his chest.

Jackson, Sabina, and Josh stood motionless in the driveway. Josh knew that Jackson and Sabina were dealing with the same problem he was. They wanted to play. The game pulled them in, but now they were too afraid.

Just then the cell phone in Dan's pocket started to ring. He dug it out. "It's my mom," he said and flipped it open. "Hello?"

Josh saw Dan's face turn from flushed with frustration to dead white in about three seconds.

"Okay, I'll come home," Dan mumbled and hung up the phone. "I've gotta . . . I've gotta go." He stared at them in disbelief. "Something happened to Mark."

The next morning Josh tried texting Dan to see if everything was okay with his stepdad. Josh waited, but there was no response. A few hours later Sabina and Jackson arrived at Josh's house. Neither of them looked like they'd slept much the night before. Josh knew he hadn't. Sabina's pink hair was standing on end, and Jackson had dark circles under his eyes. Josh figured he didn't look much better.

"Got a call from Dan," Sabina said. "He wants us to meet him at his house."

"Did he say what happened?" Josh asked. Sabina

shook her head. *Must be pretty bad then,* Josh thought.

As Josh pulled up in front of Dan's house, they saw a pair of police cruisers parked in front. The seventies ranch-style home was one of the newest in the area, but it was literally falling apart. Shutters were hanging off their hinges, all the bushes in front of the house were dead, and the lawn looked as though it hadn't been mowed in months.

The front door was open when Sabina, Josh, and Jackson arrived. They walked in. Dan was sitting on the threadbare brown couch. He was white and shivering.

Sabina sat down next to him. "Hey, Dan. What happened?" she whispered.

He looked up, obviously grateful to see her. "Mark kept saying they were following him. We didn't believe him. No one believed him." He shook his head as if unable to comprehend what had happened.

"Who was following him?" Sabina asked.

"A car. He kept telling us that some car was following him home from the factory every night. He said it was trailing him—right on his bumper. And he said he heard small explosions, like the car was shooting at him. My mom and I just thought he'd been drinking again."

Josh could see Dan's mother through the open kitchen doorway. She was sitting at the kitchen table, talking to two officers. She kept dabbing at her eyes with a tissue.

"Last night he didn't come home at all," Dan continued. "And I was happy. For once, I didn't have him breathing down my neck about my video games. I wished . . . I wished he wouldn't come home at all." Dan sounded like he was very far away, lost in his own thoughts.

"It's okay, Dan. You had a right to feel that way. He's been awful to you," Sabina said. "So what happened?"

"This morning, the police found his car. In a ditch. There were tons of bullet holes. Mark was . . . he was dead in the front seat." Sabina's eyes widened. Josh felt sick to his stomach.

"They couldn't find the other car. And the bullets—they weren't like anything the officers had ever seen before. I overheard one of them talking to my mom. He said the bullets looked like something out of a science fiction movie or . . . or a video game." Dan dropped his head into his hands.

"I'm so sorry, Dan," Jackson said.

Dan lifted his head from his hands. "He was a jerk," Dan said. "He beat my mom up a couple of times. He drank way too much. He was just a complete jerk. And now . . ." Josh shuddered as a slight smile crept over Dan's face. *"He's dead."*

osh, Sabina, and Jackson spent most of the day at Dan's house, helping out. Sabina had insisted that they stay. Josh didn't think it was necessary. Despite the few tears Dan had shed when they'd first arrived, he now seemed to be pretty normal. He just kept talking about the Club meeting again to play Black Magic.

"When is the Club gonna meet again?" he kept asking. "I want to try a new spell this time." At first, Sabina, Josh, and Jackson just shook their heads. They didn't want to upset him. But when Dan asked again for the fifth time, Jackson snapped.

"Dude, are you insane?" he said. "We cannot play that game ever again!" Jackson's lips trembled, and Josh saw tears forming behind his glasses. Dan didn't say anything. He just stared blankly at Jackson.

When they finally left Dan's house, it was getting dark outside. Dan's mother had locked herself in her bedroom earlier that day, and she still hadn't come out. His little sister was watching cartoons in the living room.

"Are you sure you'll be okay?" Sabina asked as they stood in the doorway. "Do you want us to stay until your mom gets up?"

"Yeah, I'm fine. Really," Dan said. He smiled, but it was a strange, crooked smile. It reminded Josh of a psycho in a slasher film. "Let me know if you guys want the Club to meet again tomorrow." Josh just stared at him. Jackson looked like he might vomit. Dan waved at them cheerfully as Josh pulled out of the driveway.

"This is not good," Jackson said. And they were quiet for the rest of the ride.

That night Josh kept thinking about Ned. Would he be the next to die? Last Josh heard, Ned was still in the hospital and so was Lindsey. When Josh finally got to sleep that night he dreamed of Ned handing him his still-beating heart. After waking up screaming, Josh tried to get back to sleep. But every time his eyes closed, that same sick scene replayed. Over and over, Ned was handing him his bloody, dripping heart. Josh barely slept at all. And when he lay awake, all he could think about was playing Black Magic.

At about two in the morning, his cell phone rang. It was Sabina. She'd had a nightmare too. Josh couldn't sleep anyway, so he let Sabina tell him about her dream. Later he wished he hadn't.

In Sabina's dream, she was graduating from Bridgewater and had been accepted to Harvard. It was the night of graduation, and Sabina decided to congratulate Lindsey. Sabina approached Lindsey from behind. When Lindsey turned around, Sabina saw that her face was a mess of rotting flesh. Lindsey reached up to brush back a strand of hair, and a chunk of mangled skin and muscle fell off in her hand. Lindsey grinned, revealing a row of blood-rimmed holes where her perfect teeth had once been. Then she reached out for Sabina, pulling her in for a hug. Sabina felt the bloody pulp of Lindsey's face, warm and pulsing against her cheek. She smelled decay.

"I'm scared," Sabina told Josh over the phone. "Josh, I think Lindsey is going to die."

osh!" Josh's mother called into his bedroom. Josh scrambled out of bed. He had finally gotten back to sleep, but the nightmare had repeated itself again and again. He opened his door and rubbed his eyes.

"Can you please watch your brother?" his mother asked. "I have to pick up some fabric swatches at the upholstery store."

"No, *I can't.*" he replied angrily. He was so tired he barely knew what he was saying. "I have to sleep!"

"Josh, it's ten in the morning. You've had plenty of sleep."

"All I do is watch Sam since we moved into this stupid house," Josh grumbled. "You want someone to watch him? Hire a babysitter!"

"Josh!" she gasped. "I don't know what's going on with you these days. You're cranky and miserable, and you've got dark circles under your eyes . . ."

"I'm fine," he snapped.

"You're not fine. Now, I'm asking you to watch your brother. So, please just do it, and we'll talk about this later."

Josh stared angrily at her. He didn't say anything, but he was thinking about how much she had been bugging him since they moved to Bridgewater. She was always asking Josh to watch Sam, but she had almost no time for him. He was sick of it. She had no idea what he was going through these days. Still fuming, Josh turned away from his mother and headed back to his bed.

Behind him there was a loud thud, followed by two smaller, muffled thuds. Then he heard Sam scream. Josh raced out of his room to see what had happened.

His mother was lying at the bottom of the stairs.

She was crumpled up on her side. One arm was twisted backward in a way that Josh knew had to be broken. A small sliver of bone was sticking out through her elbow. She looked up at Josh helplessly.

"Oops," she whispered.

Josh ran for the phone.

Josh spent four hours at the hospital with his mother. He'd sat fidgeting in the overheated waiting area while she was repeatedly x-rayed and scanned by a bunch of machines with names he couldn't pronounce. Thankfully, she only had a broken arm. She was going to be okay. For now.

That Monday, the Club members ate lunch together as always. Josh wasn't hungry, but he went through the motions of getting a sandwich and drink. He carried them over to the table where Sabina, Jackson, and Dan were already sitting. Sabina and Jackson looked exhausted and miserable. Dan didn't look too bad though. Josh winced. He didn't know how they were going to take what he was about to say.

"My mom fell down the stairs and broke her arm," Josh announced. He paused and then lowered his voice. "And I think I *made* her fall."

Dan chuckled a little. "What? You mean you pushed her down the stairs?"

Josh glared at Dan. "Nothing happened to make my mother fall," Josh explained. "I got angry at her, and she just fell." He clenched his fingers into fists.

Jackson looked down at his salad like it was sawdust. Sabina's eyes filled with tears.

"Yeah, Josh," Dan said through a mouthful of peanut butter and jelly sandwich, "It's called gravity. Sometimes people fall down the stairs. Geez, man, you took physics, didn't you? I mean, what is wrong with you guys? You'd think—"

"Lindsey died last night," Sabina interrupted.

Josh's head jerked up. "Did they find out what was wrong with her?"

Sabina shook her head. She was crying now. "Her symptoms looked like some kind of flesh-eating virus," she said, shuddering. "But when they tested her blood, they couldn't find any evidence of a virus."

"And the kind of symptoms she had have only been seen in people who live in Africa," Jackson added gravely. His red-rimmed eyes looked hopeless. "Lindsey's never been outside of the United States."

"What have we done?" Josh whispered. "What did that game do?"

After lunch, Josh and Sabina were racing through the halls to their next class when someone caught the collar of Josh's shirt. Josh skidded to a halt, nearly choking as he looked up. His heart sank. It was Principal Weston. Most of the students called her "Wicked Witch Weston." She had gray hair that strung around her shoulders like old spaghetti. She always wore the same plain black dress with pointy witch-like shoes, and she was so thin that some kids joked that she was two-dimensional. She also had a reputation for getting a thrill out of sending kids to detention.

"No running in the hall!" Principal Weston barked. She started writing out detention slips for both Josh and Sabina. Josh nearly groaned out loud. As if things weren't bad enough. Now he'd have to deal with detention and probably a lecture from his mother. Sabina looked like she was going to start crying again. Josh was pretty sure Sabina had never had detention before.

"Report to my office after school. I'll direct you to your detention room. And no running!" Principal Weston shoved the bright yellow detention slips into their hands and marched away.

As Sabina and Josh headed slowly to their class, Josh took a deep breath. Having detention was going to make him miss his very first football practice. But he knew he couldn't get angry at Principal Weston. He didn't want anything to happen to her. He thought about happy things, like when he kicked the football straight through the goal posts. Or how he felt when Sabina held his hand or lightly brushed past him. Josh hoped Sabina was doing the same.

When Sabina and Josh arrived at Principal Weston's office to report for detention, they wondered what was in store for them. At least they'd have to be quiet for an hour. They'd probably have zero chance of fighting with someone and causing another death,

Josh decided. Sabina frowned at Josh as they knocked on Principal Weston's door.

"I've never had detention," Sabina whispered. Josh gave her hand a little squeeze.

They waited a few moments, but Principal Weston wasn't answering the door. Josh knocked again. Nothing.

"Um, Principal Weston?" he tried. "We're here for detention?" There was no response. Josh looked at Sabina. She just shrugged. Finally, Josh opened the door and stepped into the office with Sabina close behind him.

Dangling right in front of their faces were Principal Weston's pointed black shoes. Sabina screamed. Principal Weston was hanging from a noose tied to a pipe overhead. Josh peered up at her face. Her skin was blue. Her blue lips were twisted into a horrifying grin.

Sabina started to shake uncontrollably. Josh instinctively put his arm around her shoulders and pulled her close. She looked up at him in shock.

"I wished—" Sabina said.

"Oh no," Josh whispered. He knew what she was going to say before she said it.

"I wished I didn't have detention. I wished she'd leave me alone forever."

"We have to stop this," Josh said. "No matter what."

That evening the Club met again. A thunderstorm was underway when Josh and Sabina arrived at her house. They dashed from the car, and they still got soaked. Rain was coming down hard, and the wind was bending tree branches at all kinds of odd angles.

Josh was nervous. While he knew that Sabina and Jackson would want to find a way to end the hexes, he wasn't sure about Dan. Dan had become a different person since Mark had died. All he talked about was playing the game. He didn't shed a tear at his stepfather's funeral. Josh had even heard him yell at his little sister when she cried about the death. Dan wasn't a person that Josh recognized. And that terrified him.

"So, get out the game board," Dan said when he arrived. "Aren't we going to play?"

"What the hell is wrong with you?" Jackson asked. He was pacing rapidly around the room. "More people will die."

"If more people like Mark die, I don't see a problem with that," Dan said. "Look, we just have to be more careful. We have the power to take bad people out of the world. We should use that."

"I don't want to be a *murderer*," Sabina whispered. She told Dan and Jackson what had happened with Principal Weston. Jackson let out a quiet moan and clapped his hand to his forehead. Dan looked puzzled.

Josh shook his head. "Do you see, Dan? We can't control this. Look at what happened to my mom. Look at what happened to Principal Weston. We're killing innocent people. Let's find a way to stop this."

"You don't know that your anger or Sabina's anger caused anything," Dan reasoned.

"Come on, Dan." Jackson was shaking. "Don't be stupid. We do know. And you know it too." He was walking closer to Dan, getting in his face. "We cannot control this. So, are you going to help us end this or not?"

The storm outside was growing stronger. Lightning flashed into the dark basement through a lone window. The thunder seemed to shake the whole house. Sabina grabbed Josh's hand and held it tightly.

"Settle down, you guys!" Sabina yelled. "Let's work this out."

But Dan and Jackson weren't listening. "This isn't fair!" Dan yelled above the storm. "Just give me the game. I'll play it myself! I don't need you guys."

"We can't let you do that, Dan." Jackson lowered his voice and glared into Dan's eyes.

Just then, there was a loud crack of thunder. The entire house seemed to rattle and groan. Sabina held tighter to Josh's hand. And then the basement window shattered. A cold gust of wind blew the glass shards into the room. They shot through the air like flying daggers. Sabina screamed and threw herself to the ground. Josh ducked. When the wind stopped howling, Josh uncovered his face and looked up. He gasped.

Jackson had been standing by the window. But now, he was at the opposite wall. Glass shards pinned him by his T-shirt to the wall. They seemed to outline his body, except for one long piece of the glass. That piece was buried in Jackson's right arm. Blood dripped to the floor.

Dan had disappeared moments after the glass had started flying. Josh and Sabina didn't waste time trying to find him. Instead, they got Jackson off the wall and rushed him to the hospital. Jackson had the piece of glass removed from his arm. Luckily, he hadn't been too badly hurt.

Josh knew now that they could not count on Dan's help to stop the hexes. They'd have to figure out a way on their own.

"The Club meets again," Josh said as they left the hospital. "Tomorrow after school—minus one member."

The next day, after Josh was done with football practice, he, Sabina, and Jackson met in Sabina's basement again. The boarded-up window was an all-too-present reminder of how serious their situation was. They had to keep their emotions in check. And they could never play the game again.

They had decided to start at the source—the game. Sabina carefully pulled off the box's cover. She pulled out the board, the cards, the handwritten hexes they'd used, and the crystal. Josh's fingers itched to pick up a spell card or try a hex again. But he sat on his hands instead and tried not to stare at the crystal. The still-visible image of the girl's face in its center seemed to be winking at him, mocking him.

Carefully, they read through the hex instructions again, looking for any clues they might have missed. There were none.

"Let's see if technology can help us." Jackson pulled out his laptop and picked up a signal from the wireless router Sabina's mom had recently installed in their house. He Googled "Black Magic." Sixty-eight million links came up. They ranged from instructions on satanic rituals to Web-design companies. He tried narrowing the search using words specific to the game. Nothing that came up was even close.

"Great . . . ," Sabina said. She smacked her fist hard against a sofa cushion. The handwritten instructions that had been wedged behind it poked up. Sabina pulled out the paper and examined it. There was something written on the back: *MG*

"What's MG?" Josh asked.

"Looks like someone's initials," said Jackson. "Maybe the person who wrote the hex instructions?"

Sabina shook her head. "But what would the G stand for? My family—the Lawstons—have been in this house for eighty years."

"What about before your family moved in?" Jackson asked. "This looks like a really old game. Could the previous owners have left it behind?"

Sabina thought for a few seconds. "I do remember my mom telling me about the people my great-grandmother bought this place from. What was their last name?" She looked at the ceiling, trying to remember. "Ummmm . . . Greenfeld! That was it."

"Do you know if they had any kids?" Jackson asked.

"I think they did, but I have no idea what their names were."

Jackson was already typing away at the computer. "What are you doing?" Josh asked. He wasn't sure where this was headed.

"If they had kids, they must have gone to Bridgewater High. So we just look in the Bridgewater attendance records for anyone named Greenfeld who attended around 1900 to 1920 or so."

"And how do you propose we do that?" Sabina asked skeptically.

"I have the password," Jackson blushed a little. "Remember how I used to help out in the office after school?" Josh almost smiled. Only Jackson would feel guilty about misusing the password to save lives.

"Okay, I'm in the records," Jackson said after a minute. "Now I'll just search the last name Greenfeld, and . . . ." He hit enter.

"Frank Greenfeld, class of '89. Too recent. David Greenfeld, class of '56. Jerome Greenfeld, class of '32. Probably not. Megan Greenfeld, class of '21." He looked up. "Maybe. Let's do a little search on this Megan and see what we can find."

Jackson searched every available online archive in the Bridgewater computer network. The only thing he could discover about Megan was that she wasn't on the list of graduating seniors in 1921 or the following year.

"She didn't graduate?" Sabina asked.

"Apparently not, unless her name was accidentally left off the graduation list. I hate to say this, but I'm not getting anything else from these databases. I think we're going to have to take a little field trip to the Bridgewater Library."

Bridgewater Public Library was one of the oldest libraries in the state. It was originally established in 1798, but its collections had been housed in the town hall until local architect Samuel McKim constructed the current brick building in 1897.

While most libraries were computerizing their card catalogs and archives, this one fought hard against modernization. It still had the same metal card-catalog drawers filled with yellowing cards that had been there when Sabina's mother was a little girl.

Head librarian Grace Kindal still hand-typed the

name and Dewey decimal number of each new book onto its own card. Finding anything at the library was a labor-intensive process. That's why most of the students avoided using the place for research papers. Yet the library was also home to one of the biggest and oldest archives in the state. Anyone who had the patience to sit for hours poring through its yellowing stacks and extensive microfilm collection could reap big rewards.

Jackson loaded roll after roll of the film onto the machine's spindle, then patiently advanced through hundreds of old newspapers and archival documents. Sabina and Josh peered nervously over his shoulder.

"See anything?" Sabina asked for about the hundredth time.

Jackson frowned. "Nope. Do either of you want to take over? My arm needs a rest." Jackson had a large bandage where the glass had cut into his right arm. Josh volunteered to take over. He felt bad for Jackson, and he was a little afraid to make him angry. Who knew what would happen?

An hour later, Josh finally found something. "Look at this," Josh whispered. He zoomed in on a page from the *Bridgewater Gazette*. It was dated March 2, 1921. It read:

Local Girl Commits Suicide

Student's parents say classmates' taunting drove their daughter to take her own life.

Bridgewater, March 2—Megan Greenfeld, a seventeen-year-old senior at Bridgewater High School, was found dead in her house at 15 Sparrow Drive yesterday afternoon, the victim of an apparent suicide. Miss Greenfeld's parents said their daughter had been despondent after enduring months of taunting by her classmates.

"They called her the most awful names," Mrs. Esther Greenfeld said. "She became moody. But in the last few weeks, I thought things were finally turning around for her. Suddenly she became popular and started to perk up."

Mrs. Greenfeld and her husband were shocked and deeply saddened by the surprising turn of events. No suicide note was left. The parents said they were searching for their daughter's missing diary for any clue as to why she committed this horrific act.

Miss Greenfeld's death is the latest in a string of tragedies to hit Bridgewater High School. On February 25, junior Stan Berner died at County Hospital. Doctors still do not know the cause of his mysterious illness. Three days later, science teacher Jim Richmond succumbed to fumes while working in his classroom laboratory. Police said none of the chemicals in the classroom were toxic, and they were baffled by the events surrounding Mr. Richmond's death. . . .

"She died in my house." Sabina shivered. "Maybe even in this room." She looked around the basement. Josh put a reassuring arm around her shoulders. "What do we do now?" she asked.

"I think we should dig around for that diary," Josh said. "It might hold some clues about Black Magic."

"But it's been years. Do you really think it's still there?" asked Jackson.

"We have to at least look," Josh said.

Sabina crawled into her basement storage closet. "I found something!" she shouted from inside. When she emerged, she was carrying a large old book. "No, wait, it's just an old cookbook."

Josh had dragged a huge cardboard box out of the closet and was now digging through it. "Just some old school drawings in here," he concluded.

Sabina peeked inside the box. "Those are mine. Look through the older stuff over there." She motioned to the back of the closet, where thick dust and cobwebs covered piles of books and papers. Jackson was already digging through those piles, using a flashlight to help him see in the dark closet.

"Ow!" Jackson exclaimed.

"What's wrong?" asked Sabina. She held up a flashlight to his hand. There was a large red welt in the center of his palm.

"I just put my hand down on a nail." He bent down to inspect the floor. "There's a nail sticking up here."

Josh pulled on the nail, which made the wooden floor beneath it jiggle. "This floorboard is loose."

Sabina came closer to inspect the loose floorboard. She pulled hard on the nail, and the wooden plank beneath it started to slide upward. "Hand me that hammer over there."

With the claw side of the hammer, she pried out the nail. The loose floorboard came out easily. Sabina stuck her hand inside the narrow hole. She jiggled her hand slightly in the hole before pulling out a small, dusty book. It was Megan Greenfeld's diary.

S abina carefully carried the diary over to the sofa. The pages were yellowing. Many of them were torn. Josh and Jackson sat down on either side of her. Sabina blew away the dust and then opened the book to the first page. She began to read out loud:

January 3, 1921
A new year. Why can't I feel like a new person? I got
perfect marks on my math test. Mr. Simpson told me
how pleased he was with my work. I was so happy. Then
Stan called me "fatty four-eyes," and I was miserable

*for the entire rest of the day. I hate that Stan! Why
must he always pick on me?*

January 5
*I ate my lunch alone again. Across the room I watched
Lizzy Jenkins and her friends laugh and flirt with the
boys. When they saw me staring, they pointed and
jeered at me. I hate this school.*

January 6
*Today I was looking in the cellar to find some potatoes
for my mother when I came across something quite
odd. It is a game called Black Magic. It has some
cards with it. They look like playing cards, except
these cards just have writing on them. They are
spells. But there are only a few of them. They are
meaningless things like how to find something that
is lost or how to turn water into wine. On the board
there is a silly warning about the game. There is also
a crystal. It had the strangest haunting glow, even in
the darkness of the cellar.*

*Too bad witchcraft isn't real. I can think of a
few people at school I wouldn't mind putting an evil*

spell on. Today, Stan tripped me as I was turning in a history paper. Everyone in class laughed. Dearest Diary, sometimes I think that you are my only real friend in this world.

January 8
I wonder if I could actually cast a spell! But none of the spells in Black Magic are of interest to me. I need a spell that can change my life.

So today I went to the town library to read up on witchcraft. I only found one good book of spells. It was behind a bunch of other books. It looked really old, and its script matched the script in the game.

One spell in particular caught my attention. It uses a crystal, like the one in the Black Magic game. It promises to reverse one's bad fortune. The crystal must first be charmed in a magic potion. I have brought the book home and am determined to learn how to charm that crystal.

January 12
Finding the ingredients for my potion wasn't easy. My mother had a red candle—that was easy enough. I had

to visit three different shops before finding one that could sell me eucalyptus oil, and they had to order it from Boston. But by far the hardest ingredient to find was the blood. It would have been easy to use my own, and I would have gladly given it. But this had to be the blood of someone who had wronged me.

For three days, I shadowed Stan. He teased and taunted me mercilessly the whole time, but I persisted. Finally, I was behind him in assembly. For once I was glad that no one sat next to me. When the lights went down, I leaned forward and scraped my blade along the back of his neck. I was so gentle he barely even felt it. For the remainder of the day, I carried his blood in a vial tucked under my shirt.

I am ready to begin.

January 15

It is done.

Late last night, I crept down to the basement while my parents slept. It was difficult to see in the dim candlelight. I prepared my ingredients carefully and then followed the spell instructions, step by step. According to the book, I am to rub the crystal and think of someone who has wronged me. I can think of so many people, but I will start with Stan.

After I was finished, I wrote down the instructions and hid them beside the crystal inside the Black Magic game.

January 18
What a day! I should start, dear Diary, by telling you that my parents have had some good fortune of late. My father was promoted to vice president of the Bridgewater Savings and Loan. The position brought with it a large wage increase. To celebrate, my father treated me to several lovely new dresses, one of which was pink silk with a large bow in front. I wore that one to school on Monday. How the boys stared! Stan had only nice things to say to me. It was as though he was under a spell. My spell, perhaps?

February 7
I have had quite a week! Bessie Olsen and I have become such good pals. I think I've spent every afternoon in the last two weeks over at her house. Then today, Niles Turner asked me to the Valentine's dance. I must

admit, dear Diary, I have had several such offers and was forced to choose between many handsome boys. Stan has not been in school for several days. I have heard he is very ill. Although he was most unkind to me in the past, I do hope he is better soon.

February 25

Oh, I heard the most distressing news today! Stan has died! Bessie knows his family well. She told me the doctors have no idea what disease took Stan's life, but she heard his passing was most dreadful. First his hair fell out in large clumps, and his body ballooned as if filled with air. Then his eyes began to bleed. How horrifying!

Could I have done this?

February 28

It has happened again. Today Mr. Richmond was very hard on me in science class. He gave me a failing grade on my test, saying that any four-year-old could have done as well. I think that was a horrible thing to say, don't you, Diary? After he said it, I couldn't help it. I wished he were gone.

Now he is.

Our principal said Mr. Richmond died of fumes in the science classroom. Yet the police could find no trace of dangerous chemicals in the room.

I fear I have unleashed something I cannot control.

February 27

My life is spinning dangerously out of control. I cannot bear to hurt another human being. Yesterday I had an argument with my newest and dearest friend, Bessie, on our way home from school. She sulked away. I was so angry, Diary, that I couldn't suppress my thoughts.

I heard the screech of the tires and then the horrible thud as the car struck Bessie. The doctors say they do not know whether she will live.

February 28

I must destroy this crystal, and with it, this curse. This game has been made evil somehow. I do not know what will happen when I try to reverse this evil. I just know that it must stop. Now. Before anyone else gets hurt.

"That's the last entry," Sabina said, closing the diary.

"There's no mention of her wanting to hurt herself. It sounds like she was just trying to destroy the game," Josh said.

"Maybe she didn't commit suicide after all. Maybe . . . she tried to stop the game, and it killed her." Sabina looked terrified.

Josh looked again at the face inside the crystal. It seemed to be screaming at him.

"Do you think we could find the book she used?" Josh asked. "Maybe we can figure out what she did . . . so we don't do it."

"The Bridgewater Library never throws *anything* out. I think if we dig around a little we can," Sabina said. Josh knew that this was their last hope.

It wasn't easy to convince Miss Kindal to let them into the library's oldest archives. "Not a book will be out of place when you leave. Not a single paper." She pointed her finger at the group to accentuate every word.

Sabina held her right hand up. "I swear, Miss Kindal. We'll leave it exactly how we found it." She knew that was probably a lie.

Once Miss Kindal had disappeared up the stairs, the three of them went to work. They dug through the stacks, looking for anything having to do with witchcraft. After an hour of searching (during which the librarian poked her head down about every ten minutes), they had assembled a small pile of books.

Sabina went through each one carefully. "This one is too new—1956. These two don't include any spells. Nope, I don't see anything that matches. Oh, wait a minute. This one looks promising." She held open a dark brown book with faded, yellowing pages. As Megan had described, it was written in the exact same script as the Black Magic game. There was no author listed. It was handwritten and simply labeled *Dark Spells.* Josh was skeptical. The book didn't look magic, just old. He wondered how much of Megan's diary he should believe.

"Let's see if there's any hexing spell in here that matches the one Megan used," Sabina said. The pages were so thin they were like tissue paper. Sabina turned them carefully, one at a time. "Here it is. Reversal of Fortune. 'Use this spell to undo your enemies and bring good fortune your way.'"

"Red candle, eucalyptus oil, blood of the person who has wronged you. Those are the ingredients Megan used," said Jackson, reading over Sabina's shoulder.

"This is definitely the spell, but I don't see anything here about how to reverse it," Sabina said, sliding her finger down the page. "Oh wait, it says, 'To take back the curse, reverse your steps and chant, 'This spell on thee I return to me.'"

"Maybe Megan tried to reverse the curse, and it came back at her," suggested Jackson.

"We don't want to make the same mistake," Sabina said, the fear obvious in her voice. "But what can we do?"

"Can I see that book for a second?" Josh asked. He squinted at the page, scouring it for anything Sabina—or Megan—might have missed. Finally, he pointed at the side of the page. "There are numbers. See? An upside-down two here, and then a very faint seven at the bottom."

"What does that mean?" Sabina asked.

"Maybe it's a page number." Josh flipped to page twenty-seven. It was the second half of a scorned-love potion. "That's not it." Then he turned to page seventy-two. On it was a spell called Firestorm. Josh read out loud, "The greatest enemy to the evil charm is fire. Add the spell caster's blood to heat, and it will come to life, consuming the deadliest of spells."

"Add the spell caster's blood to heat . . ." Sabina echoed.

"There's our answer," said Josh. "We need to build a fire and add our blood to it. We are the spell casters."

"That seems too easy," Jackson said skeptically. "Megan did the wrong thing to break her spell, and look where she ended up. I don't want us to go the same way."

"Do you have any other ideas?" Josh asked. Silence. "Okay, then I say we try this. If we let this spell go any longer, how many more people are going to get hurt . . . or die?"

"Josh is right," Sabina whispered. "We have to try."

"Okay," Jackson finally agreed. "But how are we going to get Dan's blood?"

Miss Kindal would never let them borrow a book from the archives. So Josh did something he wouldn't have done under ordinary circumstances. And these circumstances definitely were not ordinary. He slipped the book under his shirt. "Stay in front of me," he told Sabina as they walked out.

When Jackson, Sabina, and Josh got outside, it was getting dark. They tried to figure out a way to retrieve Dan's blood so that they could perform the reversal spell.

"Prick him with a needle?" Jackson suggested. Sabina raised her eyebrows skeptically. "Well, it's not like we want to stab him with a knife," Jackson offered.

"Like he'd let us get that close to him, anyway," Josh said. But Jackson wasn't listening. He had a finger to his lips and was listening to something. Then Josh heard it too—a low moan coming from the bushes to their left. Then the moan erupted into a series of hacking coughs. It sounded like an animal with a head cold. They peered into the bushes.

Miles sat behind the row of bushes. He looked like death. He was coughing so hard that his eyes seemed to bug out. When he saw Jackson, he sprang from the bushes out to the sidewalk.

"Oh my God," said Jackson. "Miles, are you okay? Do you need help?"

Miles vigorously nodded his head. But this motion seemed to make him cough even harder. He clutched at his throat and mouthed *Help me.*

Then he coughed a deeper, louder cough. A dark, metallic liquid started to spew out of his mouth. It dripped down his chin and pooled on the sidewalk. Some of it splattered onto Jackson. Josh's stomach turned.

"What should we do?" Sabina's voice was frantic.

Josh took out his cell phone and started to dial 911, although he was pretty sure the paramedics could do little to help Miles now.

"Hang on, man," Jackson whispered. "Hang on." Jackson tried to take a step away from Miles and avoid being splattered by the substance spewing from his mouth, but Miles firmly gripped Jackson by the shoulders. Miles's legs seemed to give way as he clung to Jackson, coughing harder and harder.

Suddenly, with one loud cough, Miles showered Jackson with a stream of blood. Then Miles collapsed dead on the pavement.

That evening, when Josh finally returned home, he was greeted with more bad news. Ned had died that afternoon in the hospital. Josh felt so upset and angry when his mother told him the news that he quickly ran into his bedroom. He wasn't angry at her, but he was still afraid of what his anger could do.

In his bedroom, Josh flipped through *Dark Spells*. He could not stop thinking about trying out new spells. He figured it was harmless to look at the spells because he didn't have the enchanted crystal. There were all sorts of crazy spells in the book. There were spells that would make your hair grow faster or turn a chicken bone into soup. But there were also spells that turned people into animals or imprisoned them for life. Then Josh came across a spell called Blood from Another. He read it and called Sabina.

"I can get Dan's blood," Josh said. "Have him meet us tomorrow in the woods behind your house. Tell him we are going to play the game again or something. But be ready for the spell. We'll have to move quickly."

"Josh, are you sure about this? I thought we didn't want to cast any more spells," Sabina said. She sounded really worried.

Josh clutched the spell book. "We don't. But I really think this will work," he said.

"I don't know . . . ," Sabina said.

"Sabina, we're killing people," Josh said. "We have to stop! This might be the only way to do it."

Josh explained what had to be done, and Sabina reluctantly agreed. Then, Josh called Jackson and told him the same. It was time to end this once and for all.

Josh skipped football practice so he could get to Sabina's a little bit early. Sabina handed him the crystal from the game and then led him out to the woods behind her house. They walked along a path for about ten minutes until they came to a small clearing. In its center was a fire pit, a circle of stones with old ashes in it. That was where they'd agreed to build the fire they hoped would end the curse.

"I sure hope you know what you're doing," Sabina said. Josh nodded, feeling the crystal in his hand. He hoped so too.

The clearing was circled with old birch and maple trees. They created an umbrella that blocked out most of the sunlight. Underneath the trees' thick cover, it was dark and very chilly. Josh shivered under his heavy sweater and jacket.

Sabina had brought matches, newspaper, lighter fluid, wood, and the game. She gathered them around the small fire pit. Josh took out *Dark Spells* and opened it to the Blood of Another page. The spell had instructed that he carry a "goblet" to collect the blood. All he was able to find was a coffee cup from the kitchen. He took that out of his backpack. Everything was in place.

Jackson was the next to arrive. He was still shaken

from Miles's death, but he helped Sabina and Josh start the fire. He barely spoke at all.

A few minutes later, Josh heard Dan coming down the path. Josh's heart started to race. He grabbed the coffee cup and spell book. He had to be ready before Dan had a chance to get angry or see what they were up to. Jackson and Sabina stood at the ready by the fire with pocketknives to spill their own blood.

Wow, nice fire," Dan said as he approached. "Is it for a spell?"

Josh knew he couldn't hesitate for a second. He took a deep breath and started reciting the spell. "Fill this goblet with the blood of Daniel Chissolm!" Josh yelled.

"What?!" Dan yelled. By now he could see everyone clearly—Josh holding the coffee cup and spell book, and Sabina and Jackson behind him. "What are you doing?" Dan demanded. But before he could say another word, blood burst out of the pores on Dan's skin. The blood streamed through the air like water from a hose and rushed into the coffee cup in Josh's hand.

It didn't take long for Josh to realize that something had gone terribly wrong. The cup quickly filled to the brim. Then it started to overflow, turning the ground under Josh's feet a dark, reddish brown. The blood wouldn't stop coming. Dan's body seemed to deflate, and his legs buckled underneath him as more and more blood was sucked from his body.

"Stop it!" Josh heard Sabina screaming. But Josh could do nothing. The spell had been cast. He didn't know how to stop it. And it was taking *all* of Dan's blood.

Finally, the blood stopped flowing. Dan collapsed on the ground. His face was completely white.

Tears ran down Josh's face. Sabina and Jackson looked at Josh like he was a monster. Josh realized how he must have looked to them. He was covered in Dan's blood. He could feel the blood dripping all over his body. It was in his eyes, nose, and mouth too. He screamed. He had to get it off. He grabbed the bucket of water Sabina had brought for the fire and poured it over his head. He fell to the ground and buried his face in his hands.

"I didn't know," he said. "I didn't think it would take all of his blood! I thought it would just give us enough for the spell!"

"We know," Sabina choked out. She walked over to him and knelt beside him. She pulled his hands from his face. "It's okay," she said. She looked right into Josh's eyes with tears streaming down her face. "Let's finish this."

Standing in front of the fire, Sabina lifted her pocketknife. She made a small cut in her hand and let her blood drip into the fire. Jackson shakily did the same.

Then, Josh approached the fire. He poured a little of Dan's blood from the cup into the fire and then added his own. The blood seemed to sizzle as it hit the flames.

Sabina began tossing pieces of the Black Magic game into the fire. The paper cards caught quickly, turning black and charred. Then it was time to throw in the crystal. Sabina, Jackson, and Josh all looked at each other. Sabina held the crystal upright.

"Do it," Josh heard himself say.

Sabina closed her eyes and threw the crystal into the heart of the flames.

The world around them darkened as thick, black smoke blew from the center of the fire pit. Flames shot up to three times their original size. Heat scorched their faces, forcing them to take a step backward.

"Oh my God!" Sabina screamed over the flames.

Only Josh leaned forward. Something was revealing itself inside the flames. He squinted. What was it?

It was a face. It was the girl from the crystal. Just then the fire seemed to explode upward.

"Run!" Jackson screamed as the dry timber around them began to catch.

The three of them backed away as flames erupted from everywhere around them. Thick smoke made them cough. *We're going to die here*, Josh thought. But as he lowered himself to the ground to escape the worst of the smoke, the fire in front of them seemed to die down a little.

The girl's face appeared again in the flames. "You finally broke the spell," she said, her voice hissing through the flames. "I'm Megan Greenfeld. You have put to rest the evil I released from the cursed game and freed me from the torment I have endured these eighty years. You have destroyed the game. I can only hope . . . that it will not destroy you."

Slowly, Megan's face began to fade away. As it did, the flames receded back into the fire pit. Still, the trees around them burned. They were trapped in a circle of fire.

The heat from the flames grew more intense. Sabina, Josh, and Jackson huddled together, wrapping their arms around each other. Josh watched in horror as the flames caught Dan's body.

Then they heard a shout. "Over here!" There were loud thuds of boots running. One firefighter appeared, then another. Behind them was Sabina's mother.

"They're trapped inside the fire!" she screamed breathlessly.

"We need to get some helicopters in here!" one of the firefighters yelled. Meanwhile the flames burned closer to Josh, Sabina, and Jackson.

It seemed like an eternity later when a spray of water hit the burning trees to their right. Then another spray hit the trees to their left. Within minutes, the fire was out. The charred tree limbs and acrid smell were all that remained of the blaze.

"Is it over?" Jackson whispered.

Josh watched the firefighters collect Dan's body. He wondered what the Club would do next.

In the next few weeks, Josh, Sabina, and Jackson, not sure if the spell had truly worked, were careful with their emotions. Josh would return from school every day and go right to his room. He didn't want to risk getting upset with his parents or Sam. But when no one dropped dead after someone knocked Sabina's lunch tray out of her hands one day, they figured they were safe.

The benefits that they had gained with the hexes also went away. Sabina's mother lost her high-paying position at work, and Sabina had to continue working hard for a scholarship. Josh didn't think she seemed to mind too much, though. She was still pulling straight As at the end of the school year, even in chemistry.

Jackson's voice went back to normal, but he didn't mind. He confided in Josh and Sabina that he liked it much better that way. They preferred it too. Jackson continued to struggle in debate, even without Miles as his rival. But he kept practicing and eventually snagged second place in the district-wide debate championships.

Josh quit the football team before the end of the season. He decided it was better than enduring the glares of his teammates when he made yet another fumble or missed his hundredth kick.

Coach Tyree was mystified at the change in his best player. "Josh," he said. "What happened? You were going to take this team to the championship!" Josh would just shrug. He took up skateboarding instead of football.

They never did find out how the game in Sabina's basement came to be or who wrote the mysterious spell book that seemed to match it. Jackson thought it was the work of a powerful sorcerer from long ago and that Megan had unknowingly unleashed his power by charming the crystal. Sabina thought an ancient witch had created the game and written the book. She said "Black Magic" sounded like a witch term.

Josh didn't really want to know how it all came to be, anyway.

All he knew was that they had destroyed a great evil. And no one ever suspected that four kids from Bridgewater High were responsible for the string of mysterious deaths that occurred in Bridgewater that fall.

The police ruled Dan's death to be accidental, due to a fire that simply got out of hand. Josh, Sabina, and Jackson didn't talk about Dan very much, or the others who had died. It was too difficult to think about. But every once in a while, Josh would have nightmares about Ned Onger. Sometimes, after those nightmares, he'd wake up and swear he could hear a heartbeat echoing in the darkness.

Everything's fine in Bridgewater. Really . . .

Or is it?

Look for these other titles from the
Night Fall collection.

MESSAGES FROM BEYOND

Some guy named Ethan Davis has been texting Cassie. He seems to know all about her—but she can't place him. He's not in Bridgewater High's yearbook either. Cassie thinks one of her friends is punking her. But she can't ignore the strange coincidences—like how Ethan looks just like the guy in her nightmares.

Cassie's search for Ethan leads her to a shocking discovery—and a struggle for her life. Will Cassie be able to break free from her mysterious stalker?

THE PROTECTORS

Luke's life has never been "normal." How could it be, with his mother holding séances and his half-crazy stepfather working as Bridgewater's mortician? But living in a funeral home never bothered Luke. That is, until the night of his mom's accident.

Sounds of screaming now shatter Luke's dreams. And his stepfather is acting even stranger. When bodies in the funeral home start delivering messages to Luke, he is certain that he's going nuts. As he tries to solve his mother's death, Luke discovers a secret more horrifying than any nightmare.

SKIN

It looks like a pizza exploded on Nick Barry's face. But bad skin is the least of his problems. His bones feel like living ice. A strange rash—like scratches—seems to be some sort of ancient code. And then there's the anger . . .

Something evil is living under Nick's skin. Where did it come from? What does it want? With the help of a dead kid's diary, a nun, and a local professor, Nick slowly finds out what's wrong with him. But there's still one question that Nick must face alone: how do you destroy an evil that's *inside* you?

THAW

A July storm caused a major power outage in Bridgewater. Now a research project at the Institute for Cryogenic Experimentation has been ruined, and the thawed-out bodies of twenty-seven federal inmates are missing.

At first, Dani Kraft didn't think much of the breaking news. But after her best friend Jake disappears, a mysterious visitor connects the dots for Dani. Jake has been taken in by an infamous cult leader. To get him back, Dani must enter a dangerous alternate reality where a defrosted cult leader is beginning to act like some kind of god.

UNTHINKABLE

Omar Phillips is Bridgewater High's favorite local teen author. His Facebook fans can't wait for his next horror story. But lately Omar's imagination has turned against him. Horrifying visions of death and destruction come over him with wide-screen intensity. The only way to stop the visions is to write them down. Until they start coming true . . .

Enter Sophie Minax, the mysterious Goth girl who's been following Omar at school. "I'm one of you," Sophie says. She tells Omar how to end the visions—but the only thing worse than Sophie's cure may be what happens if he ignores it.